HOWARD CALVERT & CLAUDIA BOLDT

LOTS OF FROGS

h
Hodder
Children's
Books

Tommy Fox
owns a box.
In the box?
Lots of frogs.

Tiny frogs,
giant toads.
Count them up,
loads and loads.

Frogs from Spain,
frogs from France.
Some can sing,
some can dance.

Rushing to
show-and-tell.
Just in time –
there's the bell.

Into school,
"ribbets" loud.
Classmates all
form a crowd.

Box jumps left,
box jumps right.
Tom holds on,
squeezes tight.

But poor Tom
has a cough.
Sneezes loud,
lid flies off!

Frogs jump out
on the mat.
Leap away,
just like that.

All the frogs
go berserk.
Screams and shouts –
no more work!

Children laugh,
teachers shriek
as frogs play
hide-and-seek.

Frogs in coats,
frogs in shoes.
Frogs in sinks,
more in loos.

Mr Fisher
tells them off.
Tongues stick out,
teacher's shocked.

Tom's not sure
what to do.
Bounce, bounce, bounce –
there's a clue!

Tom boings round
with a net.
Swings and swipes,
no luck yet.

But he's quick,
bounces fast.
What's he caught?
A frog! At last!

One, two, three
in the net.
Four, five, six,
lots to get.

5

6

Frogs are in
hopping heaven.
Snatches one,
that makes seven.

On a roll,
eight, nine, ten.
Some spring out . . .
start again!

7

8

9

10

More, more, more,
in they go.
Round the school,
Tom's not slow.

Net's quite full,
halfway there.
Look! There's five
on teacher's chair!

Staffroom next,
do they dare?
Three jump in
Headteacher's hair!

Rows of frogs
drinking tea.

Catching bugs,
full of glee.

In the hall,
frogs steal food.
Croak and grunt,
how very rude!

Tom bounds in
while they eat.
Scoops them up
off their feet.

Now he's got
one to go.
Searches high,
searches low.

Frank the frog's
in the gym.
Hopping quick,
big fat grin.

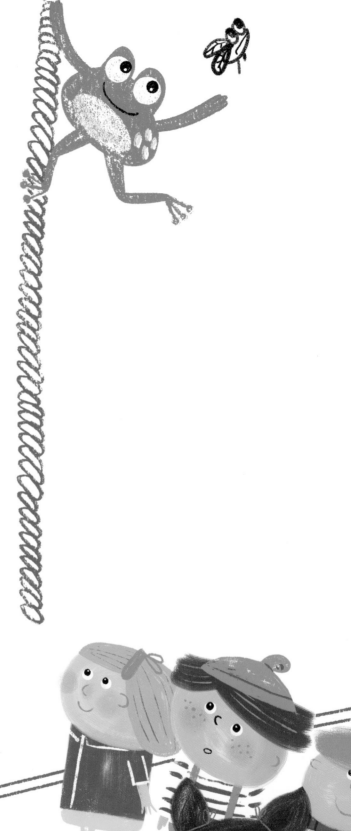
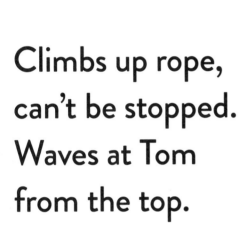

Climbs up rope,
can't be stopped.
Waves at Tom
from the top.

Fly flies by,
Frank's tongue pops!
Falls off rope . . .

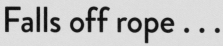

. . . lands in box!

All the frogs
in the box.
Tom smiles wide,
then he . . .

. . . coughs!

For Georgie, with love always – H.C.

For Phinie, with love – C.B.

HODDER CHILDREN'S BOOKS
First published in Great Britain in 2018 by Hodder and Stoughton

Text copyright © Howard Calvert, 2018
Illustrations copyright © Claudia Boldt, 2018

A CIP catalogue record for this book is available from the British Library.

HB ISBN: 978 1 444 93964 4
PB ISBN: 978 1 444 93965 1

10 9 8 7 6 5 4 3 2 1

Printed and bound in China

Hodder Children's Books
An imprint of Hachette Children's Group
Part of Hodder and Stoughton
Carmelite House
50 Victoria Embankment
London, EC4Y 0DZ

An Hachette UK Company
www.hachette.co.uk
www.hachettechildrens.co.uk